Tom and Pippo Go Shopping

PIPPO

HELEN OXENBURY

WALKER BOOKS
LONDON

Today Mummy and I went
shopping. I took Pippo.
Pippo likes to go to the shops.

I said he would love
a little piece of bread.

But I ate it.

I said Pippo would love
a ripe, juicy plum.

But I ate it.

Pippo wanted just a little
piece of cheese from the
cheese counter.

But I ate it.

When we had bought all the
shopping, Mummy gave me the
money and said I could pay.

Mummy had a cup of tea and I
had a little drink.
But there wasn't enough for Pippo.

Anyway, I'll give Pippo some tea when we get home.